HORRID HENRY

Meet HORRID HENRY the laugh-out-loud worldwide sensation!

* Over 15 million copies sold in 27 countries and counting
* # 1 chapter book series in the UK
* Francesca Simon is the only American author to ever win the Galaxy British Book Awards Children's Book of the year (past winners include J.K. Rowling, Philip Pullman, and Eoin Colfer).

"Horrid Henry is a fabulous antihero…**a modern comic classic**." —*Guardian*

"**Wonderfully appealing to girls and boys alike**, a precious rarity at this age." —Judith Woods, *Times*

"The best children's comic writer."
—Amanda Craig, *Times*

"**I love the Horrid Henry books by Francesca Simon**. They have lots of funny bits in. And Henry always gets into trouble!" —Mia, age 6, *BBC Learning Is Fun*

"My two boys love this book, and **I have actually had tears running down my face and had to stop reading because of laughing so hard**." —T. Franklin, Parent

"**It's easy to see why Horrid Henry is the bestselling character for five- to eight-year-olds**." —*Liverpool Echo*

"Francesca Simon's truly horrific little boy is **a monstrously enjoyable creation**. Parents love them because Henry makes their own little darlings seem like angels." —*Guardian Children's Books Supplement*

"I have tried out the Horrid Henry books with groups of children as a parent, as a babysitter, and as a teacher. **Children love to either hear them read aloud or to read them themselves**." —Danielle Hall, Teacher

"A flicker of recognition must pass through most teachers and parents when they read Horrid Henry. **There's a tiny bit of him in all of us**." —Nancy Astee, *Child Education*

"**As a teacher...it's great to get a series of books my class loves**. They go mad for Horrid Henry." —A teacher

"**Henry is a beguiling hero who has entranced millions of reluctant readers**." —*Herald*

"An absolutely fantastic series and surely a winner with all children. Long live Francesca Simon and her brilliant books! More, more please!" —A parent

"**Laugh-out-loud reading for both adults and children alike**." —A parent

"**Horrid Henry certainly lives up to his name, and his antics are everything you hope your own child will avoid—which is precisely why younger children so enjoy these tales**." —*Independent on Sunday*

"Henry might be unbelievably naughty, totally wicked, and utterly horrid, but **he is frequently credited with converting the most reluctant readers into enthusiastic ones**...superb in its simplicity." —*Liverpool Echo*

"will make you laugh out loud."
—*Sunday Times*

"Parents reading them aloud may be consoled to discover that Henry can always be relied upon to behave worse than any of their own offspring." —*Independent*

"**What is brilliant about the books is that Henry never does anything that is subversive**. She creates an aura of supreme naughtiness (of which children are in awe) but points out that he operates within a safe and secure world...**eminently readable** books." —Emily Turner, *Angels and Urchins*

"Inventive and funny, with appeal for boys and girls alike, and super illustrations by Tony Ross." —*Jewish Chronicle*

"Accompanied by fantastic black-and-white drawings, the book is a joy to read. **Horrid Henry has an irresistible appeal to everyone—child and adult alike!** He is the child everyone is familiar with—irritating, annoying, but you still cannot help laughing when he gets into yet another scrape. Not quite a devil in disguise but you cannot help wondering at times! No wonder he is so popular!" —Angela Youngman

Horrid Henry by Francesca Simon

Horrid Henry

Horrid Henry Tricks the Tooth Fairy

Horrid Henry and the Mega-Mean Time Machine

Horrid Henry's Stinkbomb

Horrid Henry and the Mummy's Curse

Horrid Henry and the Soccer Fiend

HORRID HENRY

Francesca Simon
Illustrated by Tony Ross

Sourcebooks Jabberwocky
An imprint of Sourcebooks

Published by Sourcebooks Jabberwocky, an imprint of Sourcebooks, Inc.
P.O. Box 4410, Naperville, Illinois 60567–4410
(630) 961–3900
Fax: (630) 961–2168
www.jabberwockykids.com

Originally published in Great Britain in 1994 by Orion Children's Books.

Library of Congress Cataloging-in-Publication Data

Simon, Francesca.
Horrid Henry / Francesca Simon ; illustrated by Tony Ross.
p. cm.
Summary: Horrid Henry causes his brother Perfect Peter all sorts of problems when he behaves properly for a change, upstages Peter at a dance recital, plays pirates, and goes on a camping trip.
[1. Behavior—Fiction. 2. Brothers—Fiction.] I. Ross, Tony, ill. II. Title.
PZ7.S604Ho 1999
[Fic]—dc22
2008047717

Printed and bound in the United States of America.

VP 10 9 8 7 6 5 4 3

For Joshua and his friends—
Dominic, Eleanor, Freddie, Harry,
Joe, Robbie, and Toby,
with love

CONTENTS

1

HORRID HENRY'S PERFECT DAY

Henry was horrid.

Everyone said so, even his mother.

Henry threw food, Henry grabbed, Henry pushed and shoved and pinched. Even his teddy bear, Mr. Kill, avoided him when possible.

His parents despaired.

"What are we going to do about that horrid boy?" sighed Mom.

"How did two people as nice as us have such a horrid child?" sighed Dad.

When Horrid Henry's parents took Henry to school they walked behind him and pretended he was not theirs.

Children pointed at Henry and whispered to their parents, "That's Horrid Henry."

"He's the boy who threw my jacket in the mud."

"He's the boy who squashed Billy's beetle."

"He's the boy who..." Fill in whatever terrible deed you like. Horrid Henry was sure to have done it.

Horrid Henry had a younger brother. His name was Perfect Peter.

Perfect Peter always said "Please" and "Thank you." Perfect Peter loved vegetables.

Perfect Peter always used a hankie and never, ever picked his nose.

"Why can't you be perfect like Peter?" said Henry's mom every day.

As usual, Henry pretended not to hear. He continued melting Peter's crayons on the radiator.

But Horrid Henry started to think.

"What if *I* were perfect?" thought Henry. "I wonder what would happen."

When Henry woke the next morning, he did not wake Peter by pouring water on Peter's head.

Peter did not scream.

This meant Henry's parents overslept and Henry and Peter were late for Cub Scouts.

Henry was very happy.

Peter was very sad to be late for Cub Scouts.

But because he was perfect, Peter did not whine or complain.

On the way to Cub Scouts Henry did not squabble with Peter over who sat in front. He did not pinch Peter and he did not shove Peter.

Back home, when Perfect Peter built a castle, Henry did not knock it down. Instead, Henry sat on the sofa and read a book.

Mom and Dad ran into the room.

"It's awfully quiet in here," said Mom. "Are you being horrid, Henry?"

"No," said Henry.

"Peter, is Henry knocking your castle down?"

Peter longed to say "yes." But that would be a lie.

"No," said Peter.

He wondered why Henry was behaving so strangely.

"What are you doing, Henry?" said Dad.

"Reading a wonderful story about some super mice," said Henry.

Dad had never seen Henry read a book before. He checked to see if a comic was hidden inside.

There was no comic. Henry was actually reading a book.

"Hmmmm," said Dad.

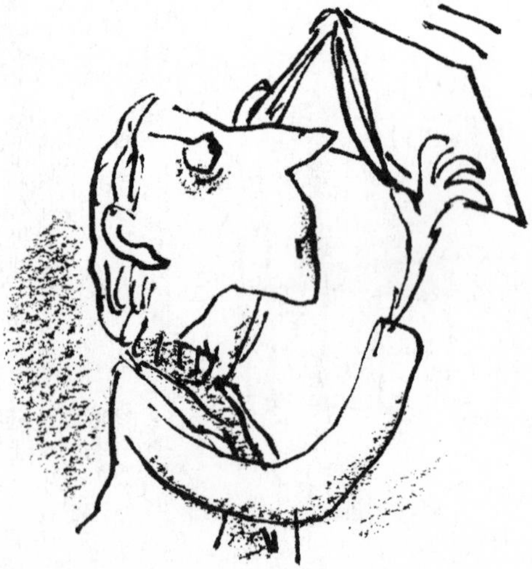

★ ★ ★

It was almost time for dinner. Henry was hungry and went into the kitchen where Dad was cooking.

But instead of shouting, "I'm starving! Where's my food?" Henry said, "Dad, you look tired. Can I help get supper ready?"

"Don't be horrid, Henry," said Dad, pouring peas into boiling water. Then he stopped.

"What did you say, Henry?" asked Dad.

"Can *I* help, Dad?" said Perfect Peter.

"I asked if you needed any help," said Henry.

"I asked first," said Peter.

"Henry will just make a mess," said Dad. "Peter, would you peel the carrots while I sit down for a moment?"

"Of course," said Perfect Peter.

Peter washed his spotless hands.

Peter put on his spotless apron.

Peter rolled up his spotless sleeves.

Peter waited for Henry to snatch the peeler.

But Henry set the table instead.

Mom came into the kitchen.

"Smells good," she said. "Thank you, darling Peter, for setting the table. What a good boy you are."

Peter did not say anything.

"I set the table, Mom," said Henry.

Mom stared at him.

"You?" said Mom.

"Me," said Henry.

"Why?" said Mom.

Henry smiled.

"To be helpful," he said.

"You've done something horrid, haven't you, Henry?" said Dad.

"No," said Henry. He tried to look sweet.

"I'll set the table tomorrow," said Perfect Peter.

"Thank you, angel," said Mom.

"Dinner is ready," said Dad.

The family sat down at the table.

Dinner was spaghetti and meatballs with peas and carrots.

Henry ate his dinner with his knife and fork and spoon.

He did not throw peas at Peter and he did not slurp.

He did not chew with his mouth open and he did not slouch.

"Sit properly, Henry," said Dad.

"I am sitting properly," said Henry.

Dad looked up from his plate. He looked surprised.

"So you are," he said.

Perfect Peter could not eat. Why wasn't Henry throwing peas at him?

Peter's hand reached slowly for a pea.

When no one was looking, he flicked the pea at Henry.

"Ouch," said Henry.

"Don't be horrid, Henry," said Mom.

Henry reached for a fistful of peas. Then Henry remembered he was being perfect and stopped.

Peter smiled and waited. But no peas bopped him on the head.

Perfect Peter did not understand. Where was the foot that always kicked him under the table?

Slowly, Peter stretched out his foot and kicked Henry.

"OUCH," said Henry.

"Don't be horrid, Henry," said Dad.

"But I..." said Henry, then stopped.

Henry's foot wanted to kick Perfect Peter around the block. Then Henry remembered he was being perfect and continued to eat.

"You're very quiet tonight, Henry," said Dad.

"The better to enjoy my lovely dinner," said Henry.

"Henry, where are your peas and carrots?" asked Mom.

"I ate them," said Henry. "They were delicious."

Mom looked on the floor. She looked under Henry's chair. She looked under his plate.

"You ate your peas and carrots?" said Mom slowly. She felt Henry's forehead.

"Are you feeling all right, Henry?"

"Yeah," said Horrid Henry. "I'm fine, thank you for asking," he added quickly.

Mom and Dad looked at each other. What was going on?

Then they looked at Henry.

"Henry, come here and let me give you a big kiss," said Mom. "You are a wonderful boy. Would you like a piece of fudge cake?"

Peter interrupted.

"No cake for me, thank you," said Peter. "I would rather have more vegetables."

Henry let himself be kissed. Oh my, it was hard work being perfect.

He smiled sweetly at Peter.

"I would love some cake, thank you," said Henry.

Perfect Peter could stand it no longer. He picked up his plate and aimed at Henry.

Then Peter threw the spaghetti.

Henry ducked.

SPLAT!

Spaghetti landed on Mom's head. Tomato sauce trickled down her neck and down her new yellow fuzzy sweater.

"PETER!!!!" yelled Mom and Dad.

"YOU HORRID BOY!" yelled Mom.

"GO TO YOUR ROOM!!" yelled Dad.

Perfect Peter burst into tears and ran to his room.

Mom wiped spaghetti off her face. She looked very funny.

Henry tried not to laugh. He squeezed his lips together tightly.

But it was no use. I am sorry to say that he could not stop a laugh escaping.

"It's not funny!" shouted Dad.

"Go to your room!" shouted Mom.

But Henry didn't care.

Who would have thought being perfect would be such fun?

2

HORRID HENRY'S DANCE CLASS

Stomp Stomp Stomp Stomp Stomp Stomp Stomp.

Horrid Henry was practicing his elephant dance.

Tap Tap Tap Tap Tap Tap Tap Tap.

Perfect Peter was practicing his raindrop dance.

Peter was practicing being a raindrop for his dance class show.

Henry was also supposed to be practicing being a raindrop.

But Henry did not want to be a raindrop. He did not want to be a tomato, a string bean, or a banana either.

Stomp Stomp Stomp went Henry's heavy boots.

Tap Tap Tap went Peter's tap shoes.

"You're doing it wrong, Henry," said Peter.

"No I'm not," said Henry.

"You are too," said Peter. "We're supposed to be raindrops."

Stomp Stomp Stomp went Henry's boots. He was an elephant smashing his way through the jungle, trampling on everyone who stood in his way.

"I can't concentrate with you stomping," said Peter. "And I have to practice my solo."

"Who cares?" screamed Horrid Henry. "I hate dancing, I hate dance class, and most of all, I hate you!"

This was not entirely true. Horrid Henry loved dancing. Henry danced in his bedroom. Henry danced up and down the stairs. Henry danced on the new sofa and on the kitchen table.

What Henry hated was having to dance with other children.

"Couldn't I go to karate instead?" asked Henry every Saturday.

"No," said Mom. "Too violent."

"Judo?" said Henry.

"N-O spells no," said Dad.

So every Saturday morning at 9:45 a.m., Henry and Peter's father drove them to Miss Impatience Tutu's Dance Studio.

Miss Impatience Tutu was skinny and bony. She had long stringy gray hair. Her nose was sharp. Her elbows were pointy. Her knees were knobbly. No one had ever seen her smile.

Perhaps this was because Impatience Tutu hated teaching.

Impatience Tutu hated noise.

Impatience Tutu hated children.

But most of all Impatience Tutu hated Horrid Henry.

This was not surprising. When Miss

Tutu shouted, "Class, lift your left legs," eleven left legs lifted. One right leg sagged to the floor.

When Miss Tutu screamed, "Heel, toe, heel, toe," eleven dainty feet tapped away. One clumpy foot stomped toe, heel, toe, heel.

When Miss Tutu bellowed, "Class, skip to your right," eleven bodies turned to the right. One body galumphed to the left.

Naturally, no one wanted to dance with Henry. Or indeed, anywhere near Henry. Today's class, unfortunately, was no different.

"Miss Tutu, Henry is treading on my toes," said Jumpy Jeffrey.

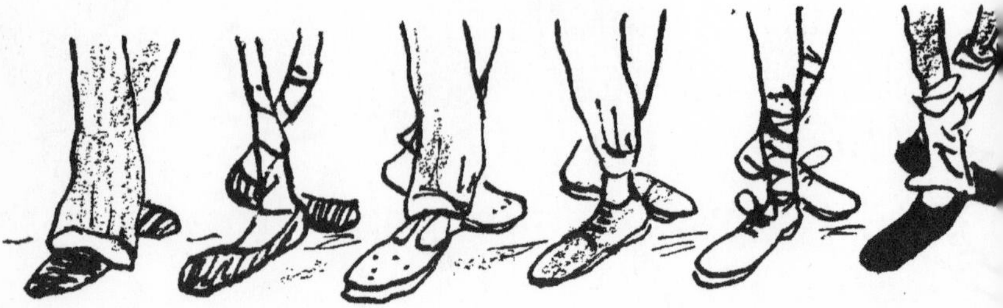

"Miss Tutu, Henry is kicking my legs," said Lazy Linda.

"Miss Tutu, Henry is bumping me," said Vain Violet.

"HENRY!" screeched Miss Tutu.

"Yeah," said Henry.

"I am a patient woman, and you are trying my patience to the limit," hissed Miss Tutu. "Any more bad behavior and you will be very sorry."

"What will happen?" asked Horrid Henry eagerly.

Miss Tutu stood very tall. She took a long, bony finger and dragged it slowly across her throat.

Henry decided that he would rather live to do battle another day. He stood on the side, gnashing his teeth, pretending he was an enormous crocodile about to gobble up Miss Tutu.

"This is our final rehearsal before the show," barked Miss Tutu. "Everything must be perfect."

Eleven faces stared at Miss Tutu. One face scowled at the floor.

"Tomatoes and beans to the front," ordered Miss Tutu.

"When Miss Thumper plays the music everyone will stretch out their arms to the sky to kiss the morning hello. Raindrops, stand at the back next to the giant green leaves and wait until the beans find the magic bananas. And Henry," spat Miss Tutu, glaring. "TRY to get it right."

"Positions, everybody. Miss Thumper, the opening music please!" shouted Miss Tutu.

Miss Thumper banged away.

The tomatoes weaved in and out, twirling.

The beans pirouetted.

The bananas pointed their toes and swayed.

The raindrops pitter-patted.

All except one. Henry waved his arms frantically and raced around the room. Then he crashed into the beans.

"HENRY!" screeched Miss Tutu.

"Yeah," scowled Henry.

"Sit in the corner!"

Henry was delighted. He sat in the corner and made horrible rude faces while Peter did his raindrop solo.

Tap tap tap tap tap tap tap. Tappa tappa tappa tappa tap tap tap. Tappa tip tappa tip tappa tappa tappa tip.

"Was that perfect, Miss Tutu?" asked Peter.

Miss Tutu sighed. "Perfect, Peter, as always," she said, and the corner of her mouth trembled slightly. This was the closest Miss Tutu ever came to smiling.

Then she saw Henry slouching on

the chair. Her mouth drooped back into its normal grim position.

Miss Tutu tugged Henry off the chair. She shoved him to the very back of the stage, behind the other raindrops. Then she pushed him behind a giant green leaf.

"Stand there!" shouted Miss Tutu.

"But no one will see me here," said Henry.

"Precisely," said Miss Tutu.

It was showtime.

The curtain was about to rise.

The children stood quietly on stage.

Perfect Peter was so excited he almost bounced up and down. Naturally he controlled himself and stood still.

Horrid Henry was not very excited.

He did not want to be a raindrop.

And he certainly did not want to be a raindrop who danced behind a giant green leaf.

Miss Thumper waddled over to the piano. She banged on the keys.

The curtain went up.

Henry's mom and dad were in the audience with the other parents. As usual they sat in the back row in case they had to make a quick getaway.

They smiled and waved at Peter standing proudly at the front.

"Can you see Henry?" whispered Henry's mom.

Henry's dad squinted at the stage.

A tuft of red hair stuck up behind the green leaf.

"I think that's him behind the leaf," said his father doubtfully.

"I wonder why Henry is hiding," said Mom. "It's not like him to be shy."

"Hmmmm," said Dad.

"Shhh," hissed the parents beside them.

Henry watched the tomatoes and beans searching on tiptoe for the magic bananas.

I'm not staying back here, he thought, and pushed his way through the raindrops.

"Stop pushing, Henry!" hissed Lazy Linda.

Henry pushed harder, then did a few pitter-pats with the other raindrops.

Miss Tutu stretched out a bony arm and yanked Henry back behind the scenery.

Who wants to be a raindrop anyway, thought Henry. I can do what I like hidden here.

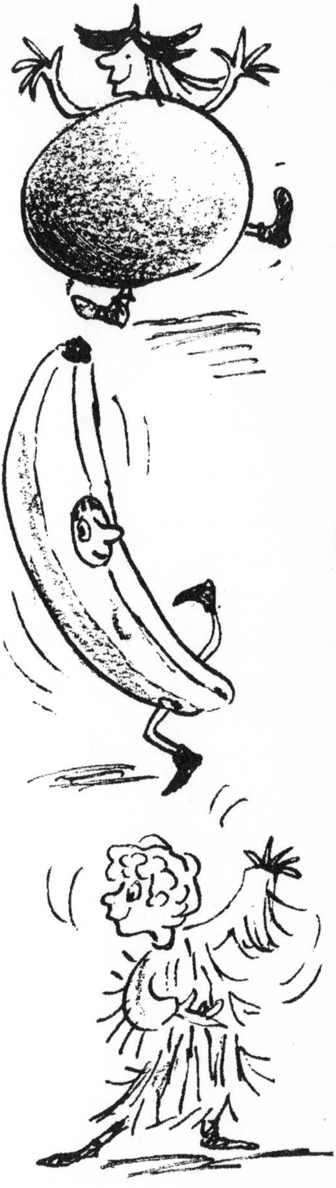

The tomatoes weaved in and out, twirling.

The beans pirouetted.

The bananas pointed their toes and swayed.

The raindrops pitter-patted.

Henry flapped his arms and pretended he was a *pterodactyl* about to pounce on Miss Tutu.

Round and round he flew, homing in on his prey.

Perfect Peter stepped to the front and began his solo.

Tap Tap Tap Tap Tap Tap—
CRASH!

One giant green leaf fell on top of the raindrops, knocking them over.

The raindrops collided with the tomatoes.

The tomatoes smashed into the string beans.

The string beans bumped into the bananas.

Perfect Peter turned his head to see what was happening and danced off the stage into the front row.

Miss Tutu fainted.

The only person still standing on stage was Henry.

Stomp Stomp Stomp Stomp Stomp Stomp Stomp.

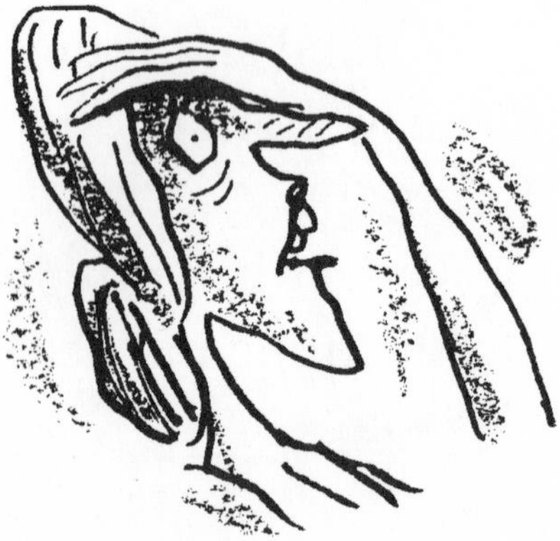

Henry did his elephant dance.

Boom Boom Boom Boom Boom Boom Boom.

Henry did his wild buffalo dance.

Peter tried to scramble back on stage.

The curtain fell.

There was a long silence, then Henry's parents clapped.

No one else did, so Henry's parents stopped.

All the other parents ran up to Miss Tutu and started shouting.

"I don't see why that horrid boy should have had such a long solo while all Linda did was lie on the floor," yelled one mother.

"My Jeffrey is a much better dancer than that boy," shouted another. "He should have done the solo."

"I didn't know you taught modern dance, Miss Tutu," said Violet's mother. "Come, Violet," she added, sweeping from the room.

"HENRY!!" screeched Miss Tutu. "Leave my dance studio at once!"

"Whoopee!" shouted Henry. He knew that next Saturday he would be at karate class at last.

3

HORRID HENRY AND MOODY MARGARET

"I'm Captain Hook!"

"No, I'm Captain Hook!"

"I'm Captain Hook," said Horrid Henry.

"I'm Captain Hook," said Moody Margaret.

They glared at each other.

"It's *my* hook," said Moody Margaret.

Moody Margaret lived next door.

She did not like Horrid Henry, and Horrid Henry did not like her. But when Rude Ralph was busy, Clever Clare had the flu, and Sour Susan was her enemy, Margaret would jump over the wall to play with Henry.

"Actually, it's my turn to be Hook now," said Perfect Peter. "I've been the prisoner for such a long time."

"Prisoner, be quiet!" said Henry.

"Prisoner, walk the plank!" said Margaret.

"But I've walked it fourteen times already," said Peter. "Please can I be Hook now?"

"No, by thunder!" said Moody Margaret. "Now out of my way,

worm!" And she swashbuckled across the deck, waving her hook and clutching her sword and dagger.

Margaret had eye patches and skulls and crossbones and plumed hats and cutlasses and sabers and snickersnees.

Henry had a stick.

This was why Henry played with Margaret.

But Henry had to do terrible things before playing with Margaret's swords. Sometimes he had to sit and wait while she read a book. Sometimes he had to play "Moms and Dads" with her. Worst of all (please don't tell anyone), sometimes he had to be the baby.

Henry never knew what Margaret would do.

When he put a spider on her arm, Margaret laughed.

When he pulled her hair, Margaret pulled his harder.

When Henry screamed, Margaret would scream louder. Or she would sing. Or pretend not to hear.

Sometimes Margaret was fun. But most of the time she was a moody old grouch.

"I won't play if I can't be Hook," said Horrid Henry.

Margaret thought for a moment.

"We can both be Captain Hook," she said.

"But we only have one hook," said Henry.

"Which I haven't played with yet," said Peter.

"BE QUIET, prisoner!" shouted Margaret. "Mr. Smee, take him to jail."

"No," said Henry.

"You will get your reward, Mr. Smee," said the Captain, waving her hook.

Mr. Smee dragged the prisoner to the jail.

"If you're very quiet, prisoner, then you will be freed and you can be a pirate, too," said Captain Hook.

"Now give me the hook," said Mr. Smee.

The Captain reluctantly handed it over.

"Now I'm Captain Hook and you're Mr. Smee," shouted Henry. "I order everyone to walk the plank!"

"I'm sick of playing pirates," said Margaret. "Let's play something else."

Henry was furious. That was just like Moody Margaret.

"Well, I'm playing pirates," said Henry.

"Well I'm not," said Margaret. "Give me back my hook."

"No," said Henry.

Moody Margaret opened her mouth and screamed. Once Margaret started screaming she could go on and on and on.

Henry gave her the hook.

Margaret smiled.

"I'm hungry," she said. "Got anything good to eat?"

Henry had three bags of chips and seven chocolate cookies hidden in his

room, but he certainly wasn't going to share them with Margaret.

"You can have a radish," said Henry.

"What else?" said Margaret.

"A carrot," said Henry.

"What else?" said Margaret.

"Glop," said Henry.

"What's Glop?"

"Something special that only I can make," said Henry.

"What's in it?" asked Margaret.

"That's a secret," said Henry.

"I bet it's yucky," said Margaret.

"Of course it's yucky," said Henry.

"I can make the yuckiest Glop of all," said Margaret.

"That's because you don't know anything. No one can make yuckier Glop than I can."

"I dare you to eat Glop," said Margaret.

"I double dare you back," said Henry. "Dares go first."

Margaret stood up very straight.

"All right," said Margaret. "Glop starts with snails and worms."

And she started poking under the bushes.

"Got one!" she shouted, holding up a fat snail.

"Now for some worms," said Margaret.

She got down on her hands and knees and started digging a hole.

"You can't put anything from outside into Glop," said Henry quickly. "Only stuff in the kitchen."

Margaret looked at Henry.

"I thought we were making Glop," she said.

"We are," said Henry. "My way, because it's *my* house."

Horrid Henry and Moody Margaret went into the gleaming white kitchen. Henry got out two wooden mixing spoons and a giant red bowl.

"I'll start," said Henry. He went to the cupboard and opened the doors wide.

"Oatmeal!" said Henry. And he poured some into the bowl.

Margaret opened the fridge and

looked inside. She grabbed a small container.

"Soggy semolina!" shouted Margaret. Into the bowl it went.

"Coleslaw!"

"Spinach!"

"Coffee!"

"Yogurt!"

"Flour!"

"Vinegar!"

"Baked beans!"

"Mustard!"

"Peanut butter!"

"Moldy cheese!"

"Pepper!"

"Rotten oranges!"

"And ketchup!" shouted Henry. He squirted in the ketchup until the bottle was empty.

"Now, mix!" said Margaret.

Horrid Henry and Moody Margaret grabbed hold of their spoons with both hands. Then they plunged the spoons into the Glop and began to stir.

It was hard, heavy work.

Faster and faster, harder and harder they stirred.

There was Glop on the ceiling. There was Glop on the floor. There was Glop on the clock, and Glop on the door. Margaret's hair was covered in Glop. So was Henry's face.

Margaret looked into the bowl. She had never seen anything so yucky in her life.

"It's ready," she said.

Horrid Henry and Moody Margaret carried the Glop to the table.

Then they sat down and stared at the sloppy, slimy, sludgy, sticky, smelly, gooey, gluey, gummy, greasy, gloopy Glop.

"Right," said Henry. "Who's going to eat some first?"

There was a very long pause.

Henry looked at Margaret.

Margaret looked at Henry.

"Me," said Margaret. "I'm not scared."

She scooped up a large spoonful and stuffed it in her mouth.

Then she swallowed. Her face went pink and purple and green.

"How does it taste?" said Henry.

"Good," said Margaret, trying not to choke.

"Have some more then," said Henry.

"Your turn first," said Margaret.

Henry sat for a moment and looked at the Glop.

"My mom doesn't like me to eat between meals," said Henry.

"HENRY!" hissed Moody Margaret.

Henry took a tiny spoonful.

"More!" said Margaret.

Henry took a tiny bit more. The Glop wobbled lumpily on his spoon. It looked like...Henry did not want to think about what it looked like.

He closed his eyes and brought the spoon to his mouth.

"Ummm, yummm," said Henry.

"You didn't eat any," said Margaret. "That's not fair."

She scooped up some Glop and...

I dread to think what would have

happened next, if they had not been interrupted.

"Can I come out now?" called a small voice from outside. "It's my turn to be Hook."

Horrid Henry had forgotten all about Perfect Peter.

"OK," shouted Henry.

Peter came to the door.

"I'm hungry," he said.

"Come in, Peter," said Henry sweetly. "Your dinner is on the table."

4

HORRID HENRY'S HOLIDAY

Horrid Henry hated vacations.

Henry's idea of a super vacation was sitting on the sofa eating chips and watching TV.

Unfortunately, his parents usually had other plans.

Once they took him to see some castles. But there were no castles. There were only piles of stones and broken walls.

"Never again," said Henry.

The next year he had to go to a lot of museums.

"Never again," said Mom and Dad.

Last year they went to the seaside.

"The sun is too hot," Henry whined.

"The water is too cold," Henry complained.

"The food is yucky," Henry grumbled.

"The bed is lumpy," Henry moaned.

This year they decided to try something different.

"We're going camping," said Henry's parents.

"Hooray!" said Henry.

"You're happy, Henry?" said Mom. Henry had never been happy about any vacation plans before.

"Oh yes," said Henry. Finally, finally, they were doing something good.

Henry knew all about camping from Moody Margaret. Margaret had been camping with her family. They had stayed in a big tent with comfy beds, a fridge, a cooker, a bathroom, a shower, a heated swimming pool, and a great big giant TV with fifty-seven channels.

"Oh boy!" said Horrid Henry.

"Wowie!" said Perfect Peter.

★ ★ ★

The great day arrived at last. Horrid Henry, Perfect Peter, Mom, and Dad boarded a ferry.

Henry and Peter had never been on a boat before.

Henry jumped on and off the seats.

Peter did a lovely drawing.

The boat went up and down and up and down.

Henry ran back and forth between the aisles.

Peter pasted stickers in his notebook.

The boat went up and down and up and down.

Henry sat on a revolving chair and spun round.

Peter played with his puppets.

The boat went up and down and up and down.

Then Henry and Peter ate a big greasy lunch of hot dogs and french fries in the café.

The boat went up and down, and up and down, and up and down.

Henry began to feel queasy.

Peter began to feel queasy.

Henry's face went green.

Peter's face went green.

"I think I'm going to be sick," said Henry, and threw up all over Mom.

"I think I'm going to be—" said Peter, and threw up all over Dad.

"Oh no," said Mom.

"Never mind," said Dad. "I just know this will be our best vacation ever."

★ ★ ★

Finally, the boat arrived.

After driving and driving and driving they reached the campsite.

It was even better than Henry's dreams. The tents were as big as houses. Henry heard the happy sound of TVs blaring, music playing, and children splashing and shrieking. The sun shone. The sky was blue.

"Wow, this looks great," said Henry.

But the car drove on.

"Stop!" said Henry. "You've gone too far."

"We're not staying in that awful place," said Dad.

They drove on.

"Here's our campsite," said Dad. "A *real* campsite!"

Henry stared at the bare rocky ground under the cloudy gray sky.

There were three small tents flapping in the wind. There was a single tap. There were a few trees. There was nothing else.

"It's wonderful!" said Mom.

"It's wonderful!" said Peter.

"But where's the TV?" said Henry.

"No TV here, thank goodness," said Mom. "We've got books."

"But where are the beds?" said Henry.

"No beds here, thank goodness," said Dad. "We've got sleeping bags."

"But where's the pool?" said Henry.

"No pool," said Dad. "*We'll* swim in the river."

"Where's the toilet?" said Peter.

Dad pointed at a distant outhouse. Three people stood waiting.

"All the way over there?" said Peter. "I'm not complaining," he added quickly.

Mom and Dad unpacked the car. Henry stood and scowled.

"Who wants to help put up the tent?" asked Mom.

"I do!" said Dad.

"I do!" said Peter.

Henry was horrified. "We have to put up our own tent?"

"Of course," said Mom.

"I don't like it here," said Henry. "I want to go camping in the other place."

"That's not camping," said Dad. "Those tents have beds in them. And bathrooms. And showers. And fridges. And microwaves, and TVs. Horrible." Dad shuddered.

"Horrible," said Peter.

"And we have such a lovely, snug tent here," said Mom. "Nothing modern—just wooden pegs and poles."

"Well, I want to stay there," said Henry.

"We're staying here," said Dad.

"NO!" screamed Henry.

"YES!" screamed Dad.

I am sorry to say that Henry then had the longest, loudest, noisiest, shrillest, most horrible tantrum you can imagine.

Did you think that a horrid boy like Henry would like nothing better

than sleeping on hard rocky ground in a soggy sleeping bag without a pillow?

You thought wrong.

Henry liked comfy beds.

Henry liked crisp sheets.

Henry liked hot baths.

Henry liked microwave dinners, TV, and noise.

He did not like cold showers, fresh air, and quiet.

Far off in the distance the sweet sound of loud music drifted toward them.

"Aren't you glad we're not staying in that awful, noisy place?" said Dad.

"Oh yes," said Mom.

"Oh yes," said Perfect Peter.

Henry pretended he was a bulldozer come to knock down tents and squash campers.

"Henry, don't barge the tent!" yelled Dad.

Henry pretended he was a hungry *Tyrannosaurus Rex*.

"OW!" shrieked Peter.

"Henry, don't be horrid!" yelled Mom.

She looked up at the dark cloudy sky.

"It's going to rain," said Mom.

"Don't worry," said Dad. "It never rains when I'm camping."

"The boys and I will go and collect some more firewood," said Mom.

"I'm not moving," said Horrid Henry.

While Dad made a campfire, Henry played his radio as loud as he could, stomping in time to the terrible music of the Killer Boy Rats.

"Henry, turn that noise down this minute," said Dad.

Henry pretended not to hear.

"HENRY!" yelled Dad. "TURN THAT DOWN!"

Henry turned the volume down the teeniest tiniest fraction.

The terrible sounds of the Killer Boy Rats continued to boom over the quiet campsite.

Campers emerged from their tents and shook their fists. Dad switched off Henry's radio.

"Anything wrong, Dad?" asked Henry, in his sweetest voice.

"No," said Dad.

Mom and Peter returned carrying armfuls of firewood.

It started to drizzle.

"This is fun," said Mom, slapping a mosquito.

"Isn't it?" said Dad. He was heating up some cans of baked beans.

The drizzle turned into a downpour.

The wind blew.

The campfire hissed, and went out.

"Never mind," said Dad brightly. "We'll eat our baked beans cold."

Mom was snoring.

Dad was snoring.

Peter was snoring.

Henry tossed and turned. But whichever way he turned in his damp sleeping bag, he seemed to be lying on sharp, pointy stones.

Above him, mosquitoes whined.

I'll never get to sleep, he thought, kicking Peter.

How am I going to bear this for fourteen days?

★ ★ ★

Around four o'clock on Day Five the family huddled inside the cold, damp, smelly tent listening to the howling wind and the pouring rain.

"Time for a walk!" said Dad.

"Great idea!" said Mom, sneezing. "I'll get the boots."

"Great idea!" said Peter, sneezing. "I'll get the jackets."

"But it's pouring outside," said Henry.

"So?" said Dad. "What better time to go for a walk?"

"I'm not coming," said Horrid Henry.

"I am," said Perfect Peter. "I don't mind the rain."

Dad poked his head outside the tent.

"The rain has stopped," he said. "I'll remake the fire."

"I'm not coming," said Henry.

"We need more firewood," said Dad. "Henry can stay here and collect some. And make sure it's dry."

Henry poked his head outside the tent. The rain had stopped, but the sky was still cloudy. The fire spat.

I won't go, thought Henry. The forest will be all muddy and wet.

He looked around to see if there was any wood closer to home.

That was when he saw the thick, dry wooden pegs holding up all the tents.

Henry looked to the left.
Henry looked to the right.
No one was around.

If I just take a few pegs from each tent, he thought, they'll never be missed.

When Mom and Dad came back they were delighted.

"What a lovely roaring fire," said Mom.

"Clever of you to find some dry wood," said Dad.

The wind blew.

★ ★ ★

Henry dreamed he was floating in a cold river, floating, floating, floating.

He woke up. He shook his head. He *was* floating. The tent was filled with cold muddy water.

Then the tent collapsed on top of them.

Henry, Peter, Mom, and Dad stood outside in the rain and stared at the river of water gushing through their collapsed tent.

All around them soaking wet campers were staring at their collapsed tents.

Peter sneezed.

Mom sneezed.

Dad sneezed.

Henry coughed, choked, spluttered and sneezed.

"I don't understand it," said Dad. "This tent *never* collapses."

"What are we going to do?" said Mom.

"I know," said Henry. "I've got a very good idea."

Two hours later Mom, Dad, Henry, and Peter were sitting on a sofa bed inside a tent as big as a house, eating chips and watching TV.

The sun was shining. The sky was blue.

"Now this is what I call a vacation!" said Henry.

And now for a sneak peek at one of the laugh-out-loud stories in *Horrid Henry Tricks the Tooth Fairy*

HORRID HENRY'S WEDDING

"I'm not wearing these horrible clothes and that's that!"

Horrid Henry glared at the mirror. A stranger smothered in a lilac ruffled shirt, green satin knickerbockers, tights, pink cummerbund tied in a floppy bow, and pointy white satin shoes with gold buckles glared back at him.

Henry had never seen anyone looking so silly in his life.

"Aha ha ha ha ha!" shrieked Horrid Henry, pointing at the mirror.

Then Henry peered more closely. The ridiculous looking boy was him.

Perfect Peter stood next to Horrid Henry. He too was smothered in a lilac ruffled shirt, green satin knickerbockers, tights, pink cummerbund, and pointy white shoes with gold buckles. But, unlike Henry, Peter was smiling.

"Aren't they adorable!" squealed Prissy Polly. "That's how my children are always going to dress."

Prissy Polly was Horrid Henry's horrible older cousin. Prissy Polly was always squeaking and squealing:

"Eeek, it's a speck of dust."

"Eeek, it's a puddle."

"Eeek, my hair is a mess."

But when Prissy Polly announced she was getting married to Pimply Paul and wanted Henry and Peter to be ring bearers, Mom said yes before Henry could stop her.

"What's a ring bearer?" asked Henry suspiciously.

"A ring bearer carries the wedding rings down the aisle on a satin cushion," said Mom.

"And throws confetti afterward," said Dad.

Henry liked the idea of throwing confetti. But carrying rings on a cushion? No thanks.

"I don't want to be a ring bearer," said Henry.

"I do, I do," said Peter.

"You're going to be a ring bearer, and that's that," said Mom.

"And you'll behave yourself," said Dad. "It's very kind of cousin Polly to ask you."

Henry scowled.

"Who'd want to be married to *her?*" said Henry. "I wouldn't if you paid me a million dollars."

But for some reason the groom, Pimply Paul, did want to marry Prissy

Polly. And, as far as Henry knew, he had not been paid one million dollars.

Pimply Paul was also trying on his wedding clothes. He looked ridiculous in a black top hat, lilac shirt, and a black jacket covered in gold swirls.

"I won't wear these silly clothes," said Henry.

"Oh be quiet, you little brat," snapped Pimply Paul.

Horrid Henry glared at him.

"I won't," said Henry. "And that's final."

"Henry, stop being horrid," said Mom. She looked extremely silly in a big floppy hat dripping with flowers.

Suddenly Henry grabbed at the lace ruffles around his throat.

"I'm choking," he gasped. "I can't breathe."

Then Henry fell to the floor and rolled around.

"Ugggggghhhhhhh," moaned Henry.

"I'm dying."

"Get up this minute, Henry!" said Dad.

"Eeek, there's dirt on the floor!" shrieked Polly.

"Can't you control that child?" hissed Pimply Paul.

"I DON'T WANT TO BE A RING BEARER!" howled Horrid Henry.

"Thank you so much for asking me to be a ring bearer, Polly," shouted Perfect

Peter, trying to be heard over Henry's screams.

"You're welcome," shouted Polly.

"Stop that, Henry!" ordered Mom. "I've never been so ashamed in my life."

"I hate children," muttered Pimply Paul under his breath.

Horrid Henry stopped. Unfortunately, his ring bearer clothes looked as fresh and crisp as ever.

All right, thought Horrid Henry. You want me at this wedding? You've got me.

....

If Henry has to sit through a boring wedding and wear tights, he's going to have some fun—even if it gets him into trouble. Find out what horrid things Henry has planned in *Horrid Henry Tricks the Tooth Fairy*!

HORRID HENRY and THE MEGA-MEAN TIME MACHINE

Horrid Henry reluctantly goes for a hike; builds a time machine and convinces Perfect Peter that boys wear dresses in the future; Perfect Peter plays one of the worst tricks ever on his brother; and Henry's aunt takes the family to a fancy restaurant, so his parents bribe him to behave.

HORRID HENRY TRICKS THE TOOTH FAIRY

Horrid Henry tries to trick the Tooth Fairy into giving him more money; sends Moody Margaret packing; causes his teachers to run screaming from school; and single-handedly wrecks a wedding.

HORRID HENRY'S STINKBOMB

Horrid Henry uses a stinkbomb as a toxic weapon in his long-running war with Moody Margaret; uses all his tricks to win the school reading competition; goes for a sleepover and retreats in horror when he finds that other people's houses aren't always as nice as his own; and has the joy of seeing Miss Battle-Axe in hot water with the principle when he knows it was all his fault.

HORRID HENRY AND THE MUMMY'S CURSE

Horrid Henry indulges his favorite hobby—collecting Gizmos; has a bad time with his spelling homework; starts a rumor that there's a shark in the pool; and spooks Perfect Peter with the mummy's curse.

HORRID HENRY AND THE SOCCER FIEND

Horrid Henry reads Perfect Peter's diary and improves it; goes shopping with Mom and tries to make her buy him some really nice new sneakers; is horrified when his old enemy Bossy Bill turns up at school; and tries by any means, to win the class soccer match.

About the Author

Photo: Francesco Guidicini

Francesca Simon spent her childhood on the beach in California and then went to Yale and Oxford Universities to study medieval history and literature. She now lives in London with her family. She has written over forty-five books and won the Children's Book of the Year in 2008 at the Galaxy British Book Awards for *Horrid Henry and the Abominable Snowman*.